For my loving, silly, and supportive family.

— Melissa/Mom

DUPLICATION AND COPYRIGHT

No part of this publication may be reproduced, stored in a retrieval system or transmitted in any form by any means, electronic, mechanical, photocopy, recording or otherwise without prior written permission from the publisher except for all worksheets and activities which may be reproduced for a specific group or class. Reproduction for an entire school or school district is prohibited.

NCYI titles may be purchased in bulk at special discounts for educational, business, fundraising, or promotional use. For more information, please email sales@ncyi.org.

P.O. Box 22185
Chattanooga, TN 37422-2185
423.899.5714 • 866.318.6294
fax: 423.899.4547 • www.ncyi.org

ISBN: 978-1-937870-55-3   Hardcover $14.95
Library of Congress Control Number: 2018966286
© 2019 National Center for Youth Issues, Chattanooga, TN
All rights reserved.
Written by: Melissa Gratias
Illustrations by: Susan Cornelison
Published by National Center for Youth Issues • Softcover
Printed at Jostens Printing, Clarksville, Tennessee, U.S.A., February 2019

My name is Seraphina,
and I do *EVERYTHING*.
I paint, I act, do this and that,
I score, I lead, I sing.

See, *EVERYTHING*'s exciting.
I don't want to miss a chance
to speak a different language,
or learn a graceful dance.

Life is full of options.

Each option is a door.

And when I think I've seen them all,

I always find some more.

Behind each door is one more thing
that I can't wait to do.
What could it be? I'll look and see.
I hope it's something new!

If I don't open every door to see what lies within,
I'll miss an opportunity that might not come again.

I stay busy day and night, through winter, fall, and spring.
I crush my fear of missing out by doing *EVERYTHING*.

Sports and lessons fill my days,
but I don't mind the pace.
I do my homework while my dad
drives me from place to place.

On Monday, I have soccer.

I'm a forward for the team.

Tuesday is karate,
and my kicks are really mean.

Wednesday is my Youth Group,
where we laugh and talk and play.

On Thursday, I lead French Club,
while we *parlez-vous Français.*

Friday's my ballet class,
where I twirl upon my toes.

Saturday and Sunday are for
games and trips and shows.

Every door is open.

There is nothing I can't do.

I crush my fear of missing out.

But why am I so blue?

WHY am I so blue?

One Friday, as Dad was driving me home from dance class, I stared at my reflection in the car window.

Reflection Me was finishing my dinner. Real Me watched other kids playing in their driveways.

They were playing hide-and-seek and basketball. One girl sat in the grass petting her dog. His golden fur reminded me of my dog, Rufus.

Dad started speaking. I already knew what he was going to say.

"Your teacher called me today, Seraphina. She is concerned. She said you ate alone at lunch all week…again. Just you and your books. Is everything okay, honey?"

Did Dad just say "Is *EVERYTHING* okay?"

My name is Seraphina. I do *EVERYTHING*.

Except...

I don't go to birthday parties.

I don't play basketball in the driveway.

I don't throw the tennis ball for Rufus.

I don't eat lunch with my friends.

My name is Seraphina,
and I don't do *EVERYTHING*.
I felt a lump inside my throat.
My eyes began to sting.

"Dad, more things went wrong this week
than what my teacher said.
I'm not crushing anything.
I'm messing up instead.

I missed three goals, forgot my forms,
turned left instead of right.
I couldn't count to five in French
and studied late each night."

"This week, I realized that no one asks me to come play.
I think they all gave up because I'm busy every day.

I know I do so many things, but I am filled with doubt.
Does trying to do EVERYTHING just mean I'm missing out?"

My name is Seraphina.

Do I stink at *EVERYTHING*?

My eyes gave up their tears as we pulled into our garage. Dad unbuckled his seatbelt, turned around, and smiled at me. I like my dad's smile. It makes me feel safe.

"Seraphina, you are a superstar. You amaze me with all you do. I love seeing you dance, play chess, score goals, and rock the spelling bee. You give so much energy to your activities.

But honey, doing *everything* is impossible. When you try, it makes you tired, stressed, and sad.

No one can do *everything*."

"Life is full of options, dear.
There's always more to try.
I think you're driven by the fear
of choices passing by.

Seraphina, my active girl,
I know it's hard to see.
But, you have many years ahead
to try...to do...to be.

I think that we should focus
on the things you *love* to do.
And make sure you have lots of time
for friends...and homework, too."

My name is Seraphina, and I CAN'T do *everything*.

I unbuckled my seatbelt and went in the house. Rufus was there with the yellow tennis ball in his mouth, as always. My homework could wait for ten more minutes.

At soccer's end, I was relieved.
I'm still no good at chess.
I did not earn my black belt,
but that's okay, I guess.

It's still hard to admit that
all those things cannot be done.
But letting go of some of them
makes *everything* more fun.

My life is different now. Friends and family can tell.

I have more fun with fewer things, 'cause I can do them well.

I throw the ball with Rufus.

I'm the best at hide-and-seek.

I'm still a ballerina, and

I practice twice a week.

My name is Seraphina, and I HAVE everything.

I have time to get my homework done before dinner.

My family eats together now. Sometimes, I sneak Rufus a green bean under the table. He loves green beans.

On Fridays, we play basketball until it's too dark to see the net.

I'm not scared of missing out any more.
I thought doing lots and lots of things
would be fun, but I was wrong.

I believed that everything
was something outside me.
An activity that I should do,
not something I could be.

Now, when I'm in dance class,
or when it's time to rest,
walking my dog, playing with friends,
or taking a spelling test…

I know that I *AM* everything.
I get to choose each door.
I'm filled with possibility!
And right now, I don't need more.

The goal of *Seraphina Does EVERYTHING* is to encourage kids to think and talk about life balance. Both adults and children can identify with Seraphina's enthusiastic involvement in her activities and the toll it begins to take on her.

Once aware of the stress she was experiencing, Seraphina's dad intervened to help her achieve balance. Below are some tips for educators and parents who want to do the same:

Tips for educators

- Teach kids how to maintain a calendar. Have them record their commitments and update it daily.

- Guide children through exercises that help them determine what they value. Help them allocate time on their calendar toward important and loved activities.

- Communicate homework expectations for your class. If kids and parents know you plan to assign 30 minutes of homework on Mondays, Tuesdays, and Thursdays, they can plan for that.

- Help students understand the value of rest on their physical and mental performance. Allow times for rest and/or meditation during the school day.

Tips for Parents

- Block time for important things and set boundaries on your family calendar. How much time for homework? How many hours for activities? Dinner? Rest? Family time? Make sure every minute isn't scheduled, though. You'll want to leave room for adventure!

- Have a weekly meeting to review the family calendar and involve your children. They will feel empowered and more aware of the impact of activities across all family members.

- Show kids through your actions that life balance is important. If you are stressed and overscheduled, chances are, they will be, too.

- View each change in season as an opportunity to re-evaluate family commitments. A fun way to do this is to make a Stop-Start-Continue list with your kids.

- Teach your kids to say "no" to opportunities and activities that could lead to an unbalanced life. Allow them to choose, for example, swimming OR marching band, but not both.